D0574229

Cinderella

PAUL GALDONE

⌘ A FOLK TALE CLASSIC ⌘

Houghton Mifflin Harcourt

Boston   New York

For Thordis

Copyright © 1978 by Paul Galdone

All rights reserved. Published in the United States by HMH Books, an imprint of
Houghton Mifflin Harcourt Publishing Company. Originally published in hardcover
in the United States by the McGraw-Hill Companies, 1978.

For information about permission to reproduce selections from this book, write to
Permissions, Houghton Mifflin Harcourt Publishing Company, 215 Park Avenue
South, New York, New York 10003.

www.hmhco.com

Library of Congress Cataloging-in-Publication Control Number 78-7614

ISBN: 978-0-547-98867-2 paper over board

Manufactured in China
SCP 10 9 8 7 6 5 4 3

4500534773

Once there lived a nobleman who, after his first wife died, took for his second wife the haughtiest and proudest woman in the land. She had two daughters who were just like her. The nobleman himself had a daughter, who was sweet and kind as her own mother had been.

The stepmother was jealous of her husband's daughter, for the girl's goodness made her own daughters seem even more unpleasant. The stepmother commanded the girl to clean the house and wait on her and her daughters morning and night.

While the girl slept in the attic on a straw mat, her stepsisters had
fine rooms with soft beds and tall mirrors in which they could admire
themselves from head to foot.

She suffered all patiently, never complaining to her father. When her daily work was done, she would rest by the chimney among the ashes, and so her sisters gave her the nickname Cinderella.

Cinderella, in her shabby clothes, was far more beautiful than her richly dressed stepsisters.

That year the King's son gave a ball and invited all the notables from far and near, including Cinderella's stepsisters. They were soon busy choosing the gowns, petticoats, and headdresses that would be most becoming on them. This made more work for Cinderella, for it was she who did their mending and ironing.

At last the great day arrived. The stepsisters' hair was arranged in the most fashionable styles, with ribbons from the best shops. The stepsisters called Cinderella for advice since they trusted her help in making them look their best.

While she waited on them they asked, "Cinderella, would you not like to go to the ball?"

"Oh, you are making fun of me," she replied. "It is not a place for such as I."

"You are right," they said. "People would laugh to see a cinder-maid at the ball!"

Cinderella was too sweet to be angry with them, but as she watched them set out for the ball, she could no longer hold back her tears.

Suddenly her godmother, who was a fairy, appeared. "What is the matter, child?" she asked.

"I wish . . . I wish I could . . ." was all Cinderella could say through her sobs.

"You wish you could go to the ball, isn't that so?"
"Yes," Cinderella agreed, and sighed sadly.

"Well," said the godmother, "just be a good girl, and I will see that you go. First," she said, "run into the garden and bring me a pumpkin." Cinderella hurried to find one and brought it to her godmother, who struck it with her wand. Instantly, it turned into a fine golden coach.

Then her godmother opened the mousetrap and released six
live mice. She gently tapped each one with her wand.

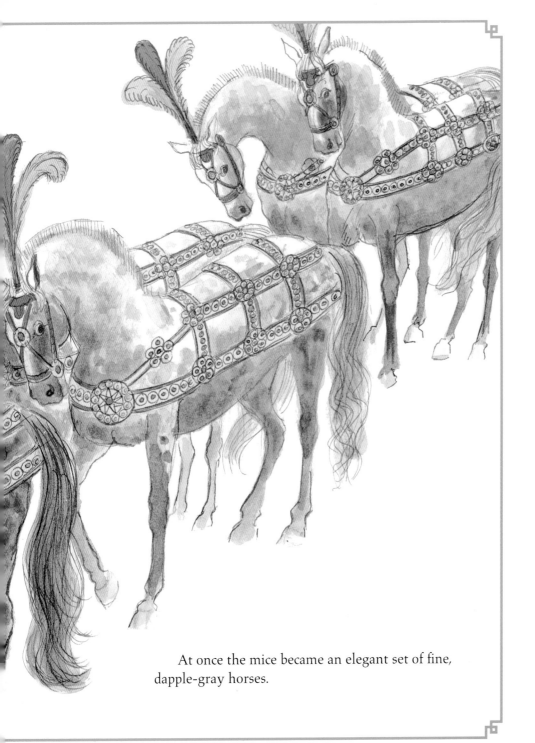

At once the mice became an elegant set of fine,
dapple-gray horses.

"Now I must find something to change into a coachman," said the godmother.

Cinderella brought out the rat trap, and in it were three huge rats. The godmother chose the one with the longest whiskers, and when she touched it with her wand it became a fat, jolly coachman who had the smartest mustache ever to be seen.

"Now," she said to Cinderella, "go to the garden, child, and bring me the six lizards hiding behind the watering pot."

The lizards were turned into footmen, dressed in gleaming livery, and they stood in position around the coach as if they had been doing nothing else all their lives.

The godmother then said to Cinderella: "Now you have a coach fit to carry you to the ball. Aren't you pleased?"

"Oh, yes!" cried Cinderella. "But can I go there as I am, in these nasty rags?"

Her godmother waved her wand over Cinderella, and turned her tattered clothes into a gown set with sparkling jewels. Her shoes were a pair of glass slippers, the prettiest in the world.

Cinderella's godmother warned, "You must leave the ball before midnight, or the coach will once again be a pumpkin; the horses, mice; the footmen, lizards; the coachman, a rat; and your clothes will become rags as before."

"I promise, dear godmother." And Cinderella set out for the palace, bursting with joy.

When Cinderella arrived at the ball, the King's son was told of the great princess whom nobody knew. He hurried to help her alight from the coach and led her into the great hall. The dancing stopped, the musicians ceased to play, and a murmur arose: "How beautiful she is!"

The King whispered to the Queen that it had been a long time since he had seen a girl so lovely. The men were fascinated by her beauty. The ladies studied her clothes so that they could have some made just like them.

The Prince asked Cinderella to dance with him. She was so graceful that the company admired her more and more. Cinderella sat next to the Prince at dinner, but he was so absorbed by their conversation that he did not eat a bite.

After dinner, Cinderella sat and spoke pleasantly with her sisters. She graciously shared some of the fruit the Prince had given her. They did not recognize their shabby stepsister at all. When the clock struck a quarter to twelve, Cinderella curtsied deeply and hurried away as fast as she could.

When she got home, Cinderella thanked her fairy godmother and said the Prince had begged her to come again to another ball the following night.

Before her godmother could say anything, her two stepsisters arrived. "How long you have stayed!" Cinderella said, yawning and rubbing her eyes as if she had just awakened.

"If you had been at the ball," said one of the sisters, "you would not have felt sleepy. A beautiful princess came there, one of the loveliest ever seen! She was so polite and even visited with us! But her name is a mystery. The Prince would give anything to know who she is."

Cinderella was secretly delighted.

She smiled and said, "The princess must have been very beautiful indeed. How fortunate you have been. Oh please, couldn't you lend me a plain gown so I might go to the ball and see her too?"

"Well, really!" cried her haughty stepsister. "Lend my clothes to a dirty cinder-grub like you? I'd be a fool."

Cinderella had expected such an answer.

The next day the two sisters were again at the ball. So was Cinderella. The Prince spoke so kindly to her and stayed by her side all night. Cinderella forgot all about her godmother's warning.

Suddenly, she heard the clock striking midnight.

She fled from the ballroom. The Prince followed her, but all he found was one of her little glass slippers. The guards at the palace gates had seen no one leave but a girl in ragged work clothes.

Cinderella arrived home quite out of breath. Nothing at all of her finery was left but the mate of the slipper she had lost.

When the sisters returned from the ball, Cinderella asked if the fine lady had been there. They told her yes, but at the stroke of midnight, she fled in such haste that she had dropped one of her little glass slippers, the prettiest in the world.

The Prince had picked it up and sat gazing at it for the rest of the night.

"He must be deeply in love with the beautiful princess," said the younger stepsister.

Which was true, for a few days later the King's herald read a proclamation that the King's son would marry the girl whose foot the slipper fit.

The Prince's messengers went about trying the slipper on all the women in the land. It was even brought to the two stepsisters. Neither could force her foot into the slipper. Finally, Cinderella laughed and said, "Why not let me see if it will fit me?"

The sisters sneered, but the King's messenger said it was only fair. As he placed the slipper on her small foot, he saw that it fitted as snugly as if it had been made of wax. Then to the amazement of the sisters, Cinderella drew the other slipper from her pocket.

Suddenly Cinderella's godmother appeared and turned her rags into a gown even more magnificent than the ones she had worn before.

The two sisters begged Cinderella's pardon for treating her so badly. Cinderella hugged them and said she still loved them with all her heart and asked them to always love her.

Cinderella was taken to the young Prince and a few days later they were married. Cinderella, who was as good as she was beautiful, brought her two stepsisters to live at the palace as well, and soon they married two great lords of the court.